The ADVENTURES of the boy who couldn't sit still

LIAM GOES TO SCHOOL

BY JM DANIELE

For my Son

You've always had the power within you.

Hi, I'm Liam! I am 8 years old. When I was only 5, I found out I have ADHD. I would like to take you on that journey with me. My mom says my mind is like a race car. If I go too fast, I won't get very far. BUT—if I focus and find a steady pace, I can do anything...I can win the race!

Help me stay on the right track and find all the race cars, from front to back.

How many cars can you see? Our Journey is about to begin. Are you ready?? 123...

Every night, I have Millions of ideas that float in my head,

So many ideas that it is kind of hard for me to go to bed.

Most times, I like to be super silly and play, But right now, I need to get some sleep because tomorrow is the BIG day!

My brain keeps spinning with adventures, ideas, and noises.

All of these things make it really hard to make good choices.

Okay friends, today is my first DAY.

I AM STARTING 5K!

I put on my backpack and head for the front door.

I'm a little **NERVOUS** because I have never been to school before.

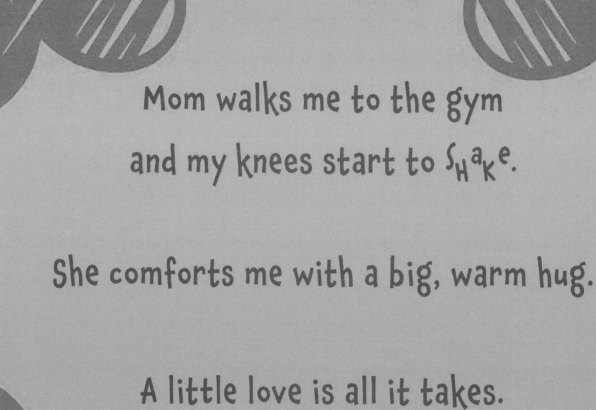

Mom walks me to the gym
and my knees start to SHaKe.

She comforts me with a big, warm hug.

A little love is all it takes.

After Mom leaves for the day,
I spot my buddy, TJ.

I bolt to give him a hug,
but I was so fast my hug was
more of a shove.

The bell rings. The teacher tells our class to lineup and i heip TJ stand up.

In my classroom I have to sit at my desk and be very still.

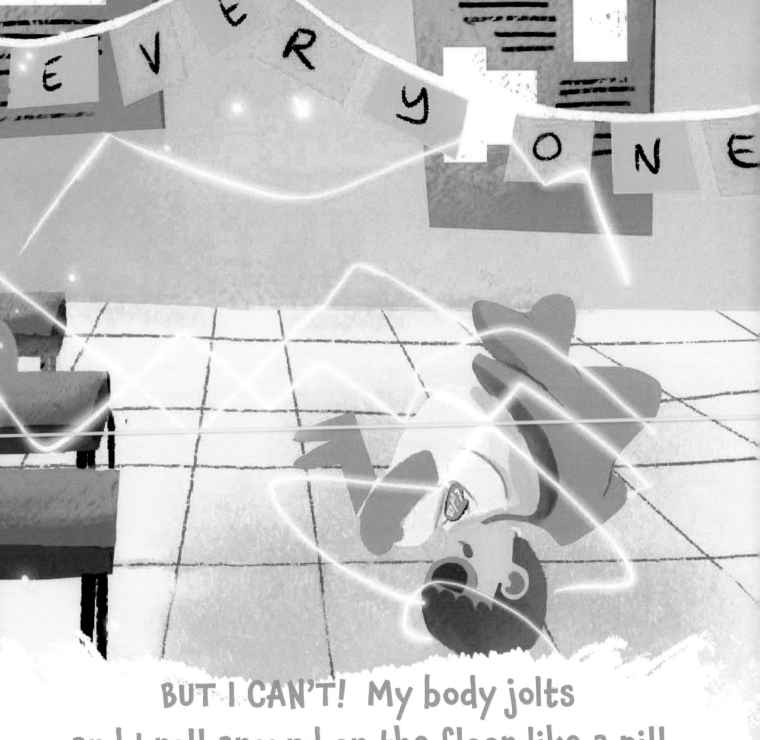

BUT I CAN'T! My body jolts
and I roll around on the floor like a pill.

The kids are laughing, the teacher is mad.

I don't understand. Am I funny or am I bad?

Now it's lunch! yeah!
I get to get out all my Wiggles!

So, I dance, sing, juggle food,
and try to make my friends giggle.

Some kids laugh and some
don't like what I do.

Sometimes I just want to be
like TJ, Jonah or Sue.

I want to do well at school, this I pray.

I like learning, but in my own special way.

Later that day, the JOLT hits me again

and I make a run for the gym...

UH OH!

There is the principal,

I don't like the looks of him!

Principal Patterson calls my mom at home.

Will I get in trouble?

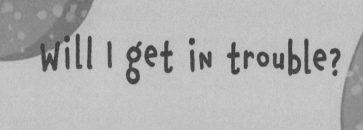

Will she tell Dad?

Mom comes and tells me
to dry my tears, it's not all bad.

Mom says we are going on an adventure and we will go through this together.

I wonder if this adventure is something that lasts forever.

Come and join me, my friends.
Where adventure begins
and there is no end.

Your Friend,

Liam G.

Note to Parents:

In a sea of books, you have chosen to read ours—thank you!

Getting Liam ready for his first day of school was an exciting time. Like so many parents before us, we shopped for back to school clothes, bought the school supplies, and helped calm any last-minute fears he shared. As is the case with most parents, we couldn't believe the day had already arrived. We dreamed about his future and the things he would learn and who he would grow to be.

Shortly after school began, we started getting reports from his teacher, Liam was having a hard time. We consulted the best doctors, therapists, specialists...you name it. Everyone agreed and he was diagnosed with ADHD.

We were against medicating him at such a young age, but we knew he needed help and we had no idea how to make things better for him. Finally, we realized there was no secret trick or pill or doctor that could solve all his problems.

In fact, why would we do that anyway? Solve all his problems? That would be a disservice to his growth. We began to ask ourselves, how could we learn to dance in the rain and help him grow?

That's when we started crafting these stories that are based on real events. I hope you follow our journey as we go to school, the doctor, dentist, and many more. As we travel through these stories you will notice Liam's transformation from a scared, anxious little boy to a super-kid who stands up for truth and peace. He finds his inner "super" powers and becomes the hero to his own story.

If you want to follow me, Liam G.,

look for my next book,

Liam Goes to the Doctor.

Made in the USA
Middletown, DE
22 December 2020